CUMBRIA LIBRARIES
3 8003 04848 6344

KT-425-539

This book belongs to

For Ben and Ollie

OXFORD
UNIVERSITY PRESS

Great Clarendon Street, Oxford OX2 6DP

Oxford University Press is a department of the University of Oxford. It furthers the University's objective of excellence in research, scholarship, and education by publishing worldwide in Oxford New York Auckland Cape Town Dar es Salaam Hong Kong Karachi Kuala Lumpur Madrid Melbourne Mexico City Nairobi New Delhi Shanghai Taipei Toronto

With offices in Argentina Austria Brazil Chile Czech Republic France Greece Guatemala Hungary Italy Japan Poland Portugal Singapore South Korea Switzerland Thailand Turkey Ukraine Vietnam

Oxford is a registered trade mark of Oxford University Press in the UK and in certain other countries

First published in 2018

British Library Cataloguing in Publication Data
Data available

ISBN: 978-0-19-274977-2 (paperback)

10 9 8 7 6 5 4 3 2 1

Printed in China

Paper used in the production of this book is a natural, recyclableproduct made from wood grown in sustainable forests. The manufacturing process conforms to the environmental regulations of the country of origin.

Visit www.richardbyrne.co.uk

THE CASE OF THE RED-BOTTOMED ROBBER!

Richard BYRNE

OXFORD
UNIVERSITY PRESS

The young chalks were having a fabulous time at the chalkboard when Mrs Red called them in for . . .

...LUNCH!

When the chalks came back from lunch
they got a real shock.

ALL THE FLOWERS HAVE GONE!

The chalks started a new drawing but this time Mrs Red also drew a big red fence.

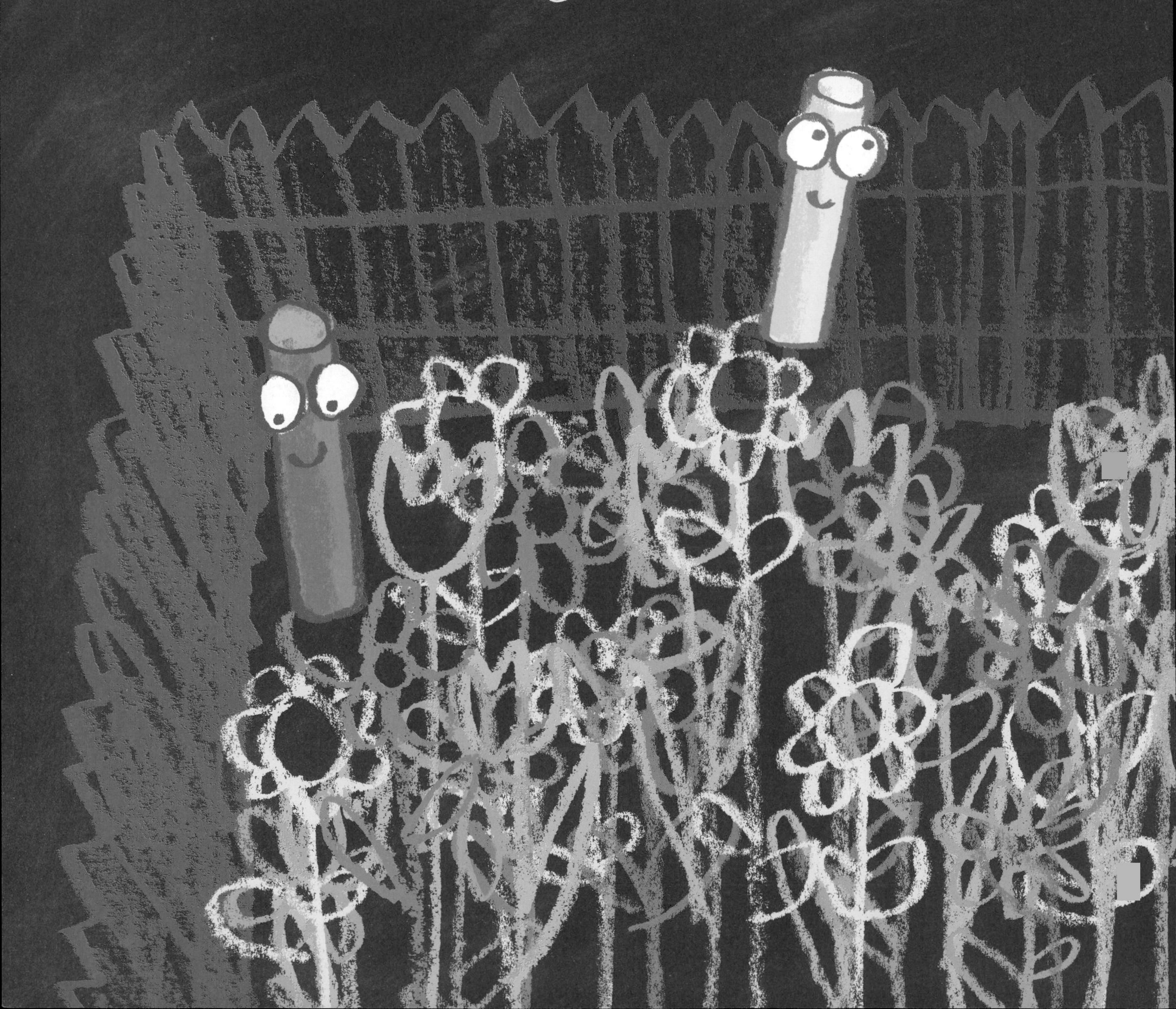

‘That should keep the flowers safe while we go in for a story,’ she said.

But it didn't.
The flowers had disappeared **AGAIN!**

And this time the fence had gone, too!

SOMEONE IS
STEALING
OUR DRAWINGS!

Sergeant Blue arrived
to investigate . . .

. . . and quickly noted some crucial evidence.

'The culprit is this tall . . .

. . . and VERY dusty!'

So he rounded up some
suspicious-looking characters.

'Too thin . . .

Too small . . .

Too pointy . . .

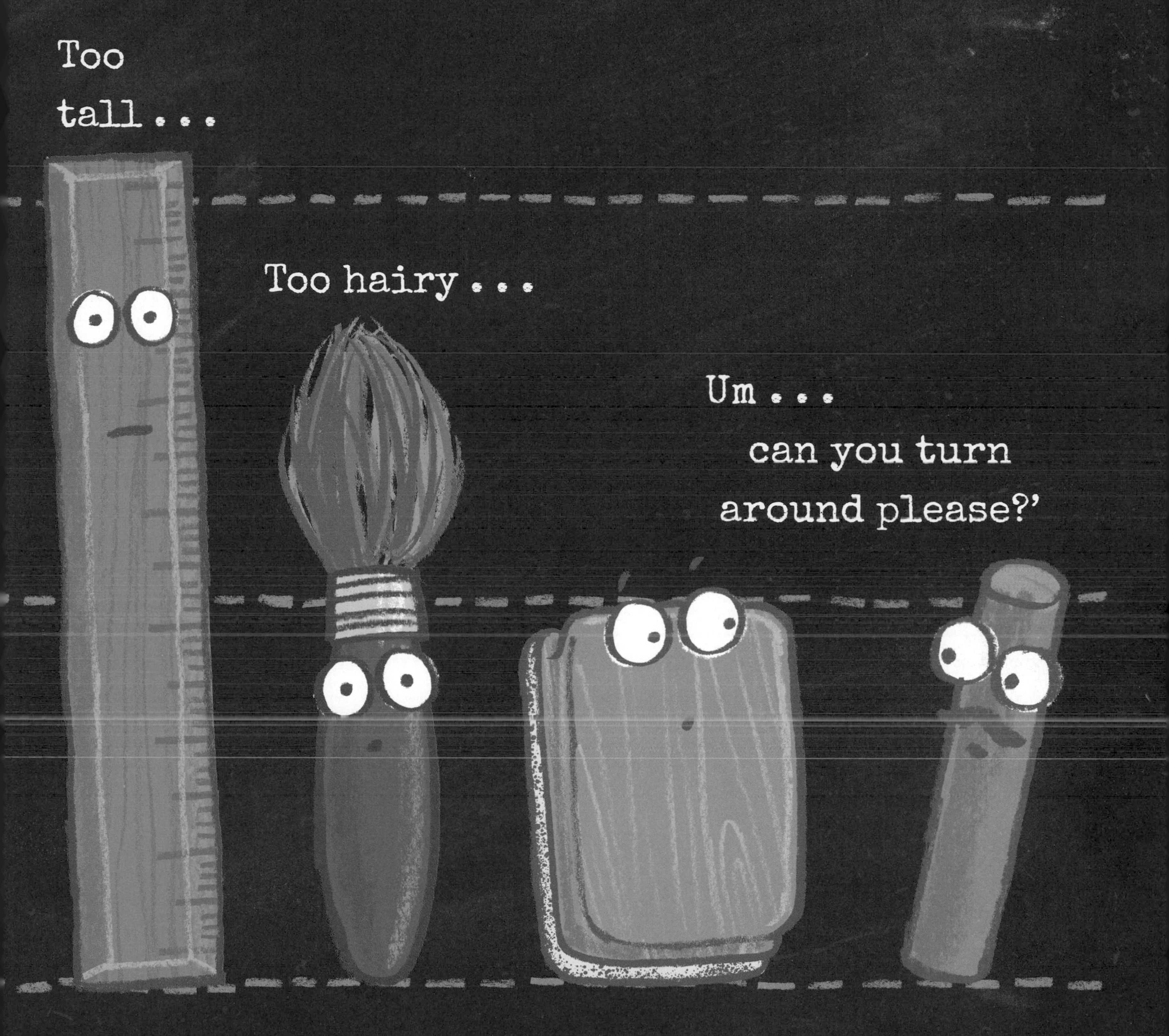

Too
tall . . .

Too hairy . . .

Um . . .
can you turn
around please?’

GLUE

HE'S GOT A
DUSTY RED
BOTTOM!

Case closed!

But before Sergeant Blue could put the culprit in prison . . .

. . . the robber fled in a cloud of dust.

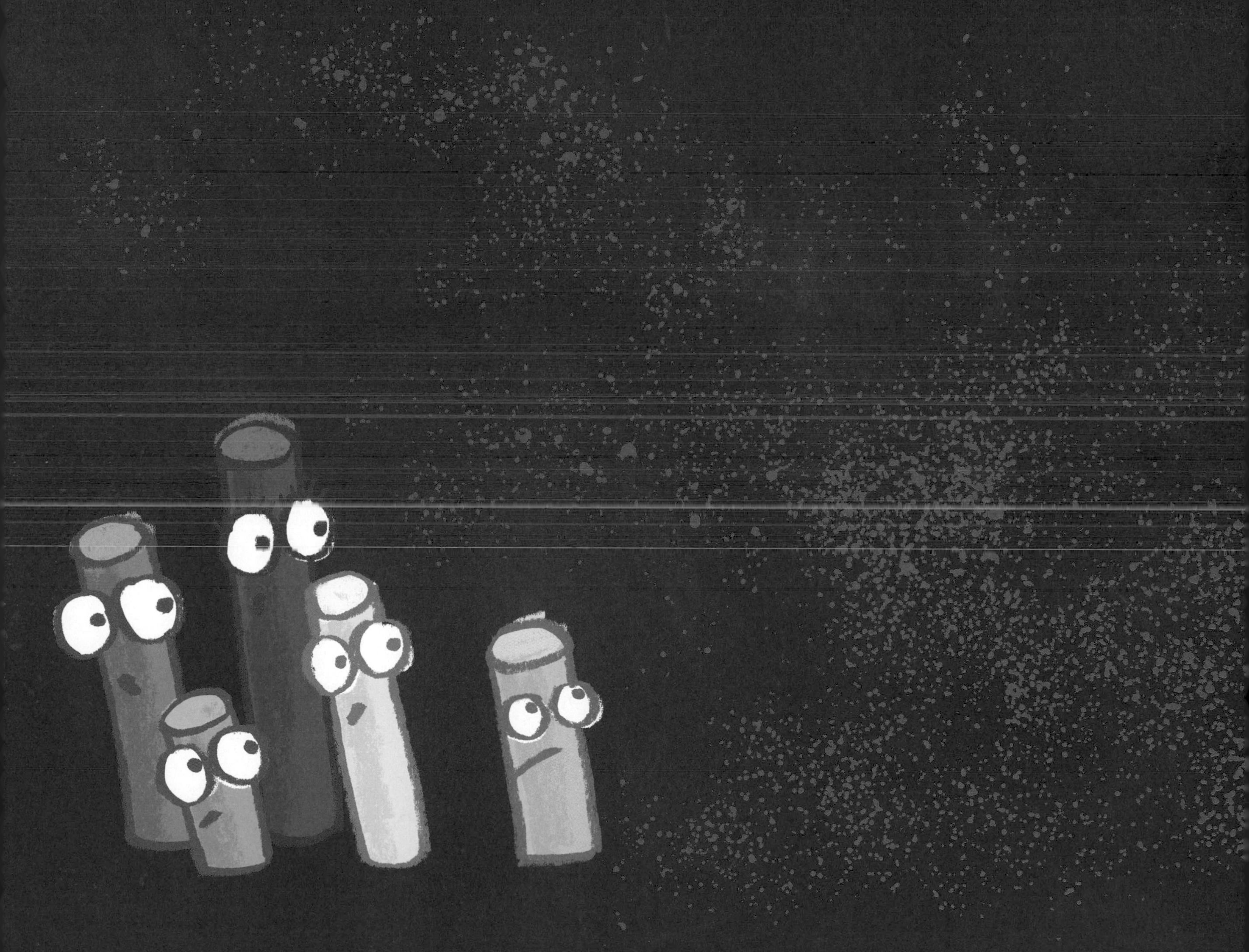

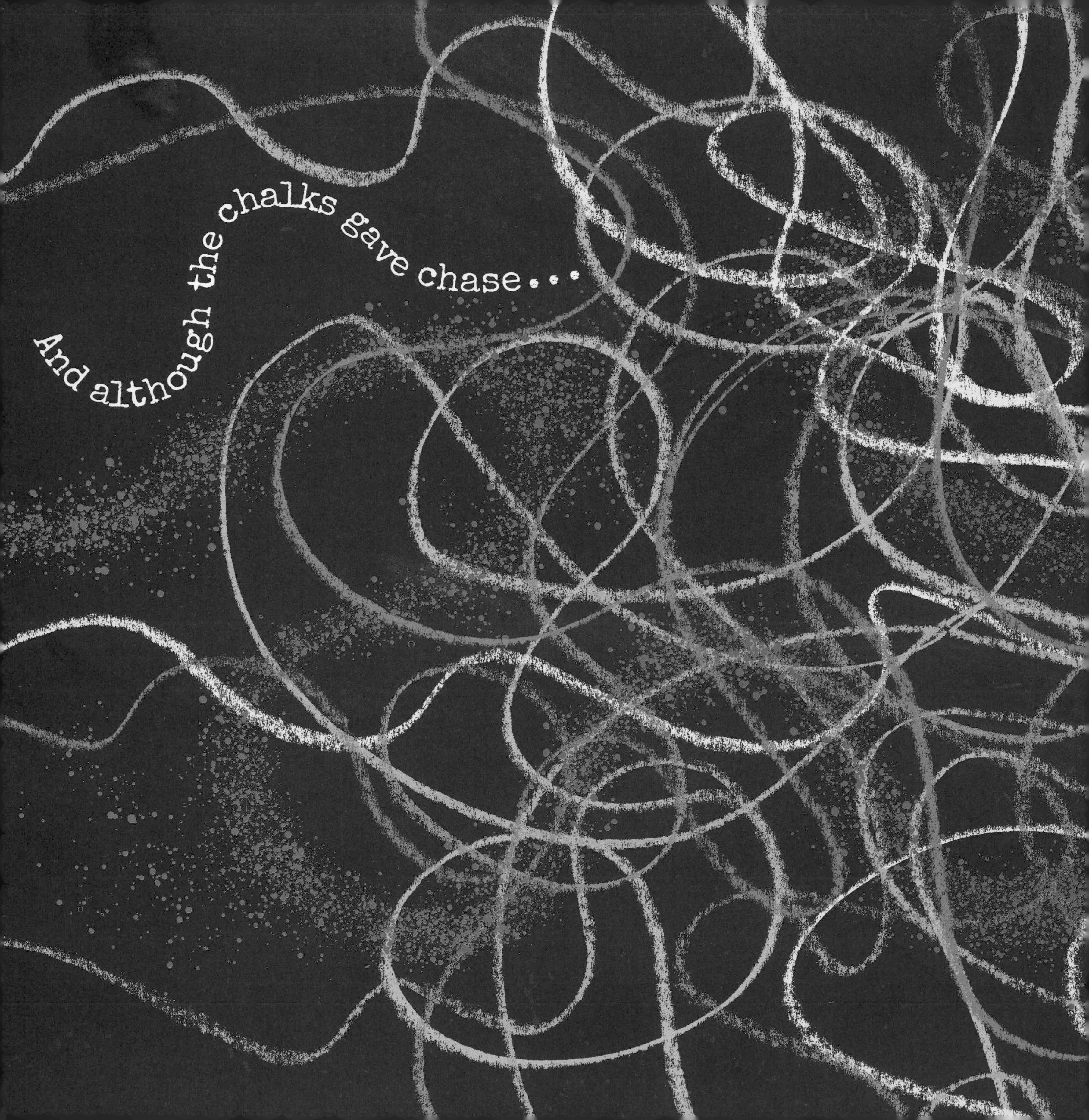
And although the chalks gave chase . . .

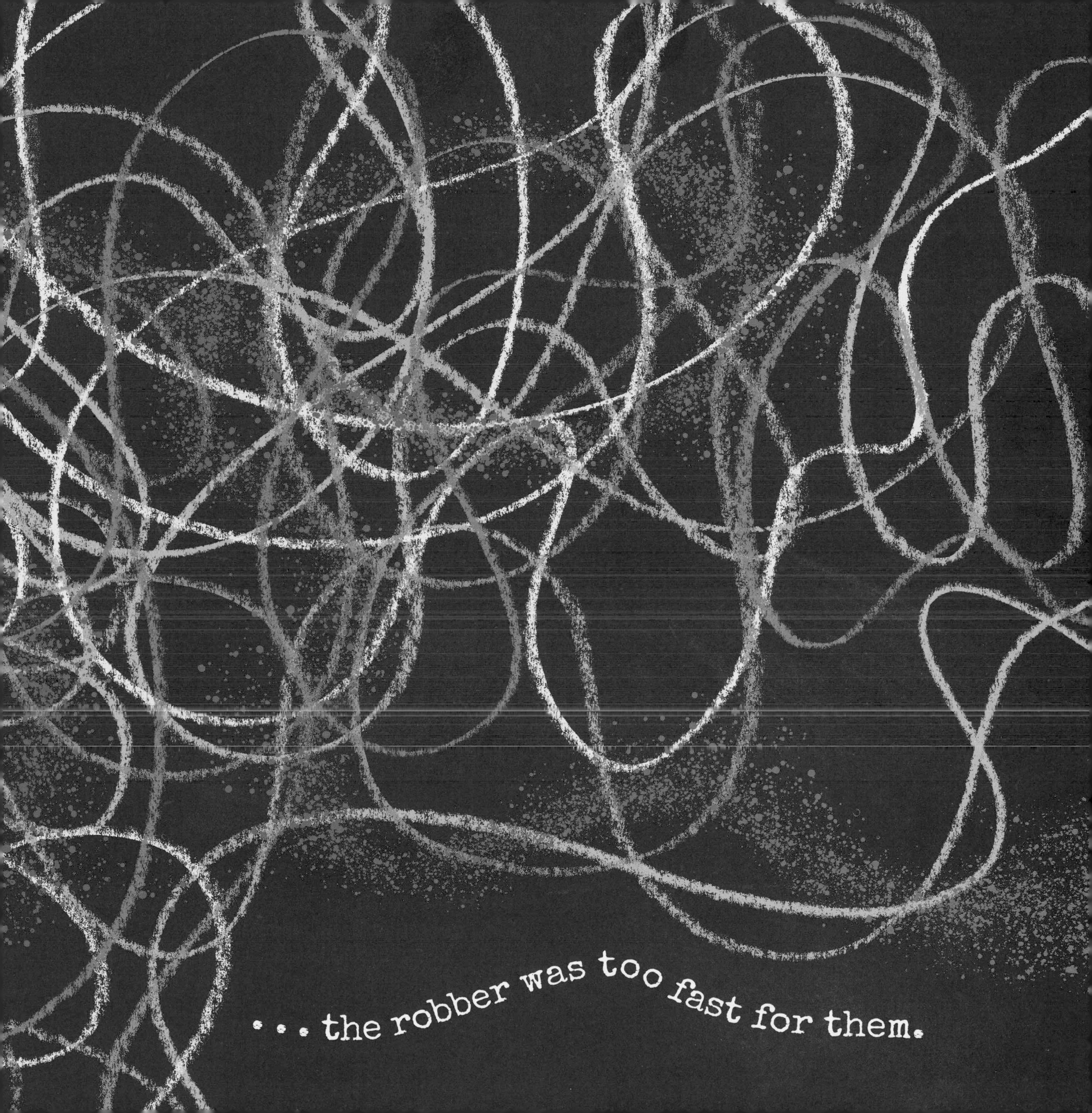

. . . the robber was too fast for them.

The chalks had no idea how they were going to catch the elusive robber . . .

. . . but fortunately
Sergeant Blue had a plan.

The robber was sure he had given the chalks the slip. Then he stumbled across a very tempting new drawing.

The chalks suddenly leapt out from their hiding places.

The chalkboard duster felt wrongly accused.

The chalks felt very guilty. They had made a terrible mistake.

Sergeant Blue knew how to put things right. They should all chase the duster again . . .

. . . but this time

just for fun!

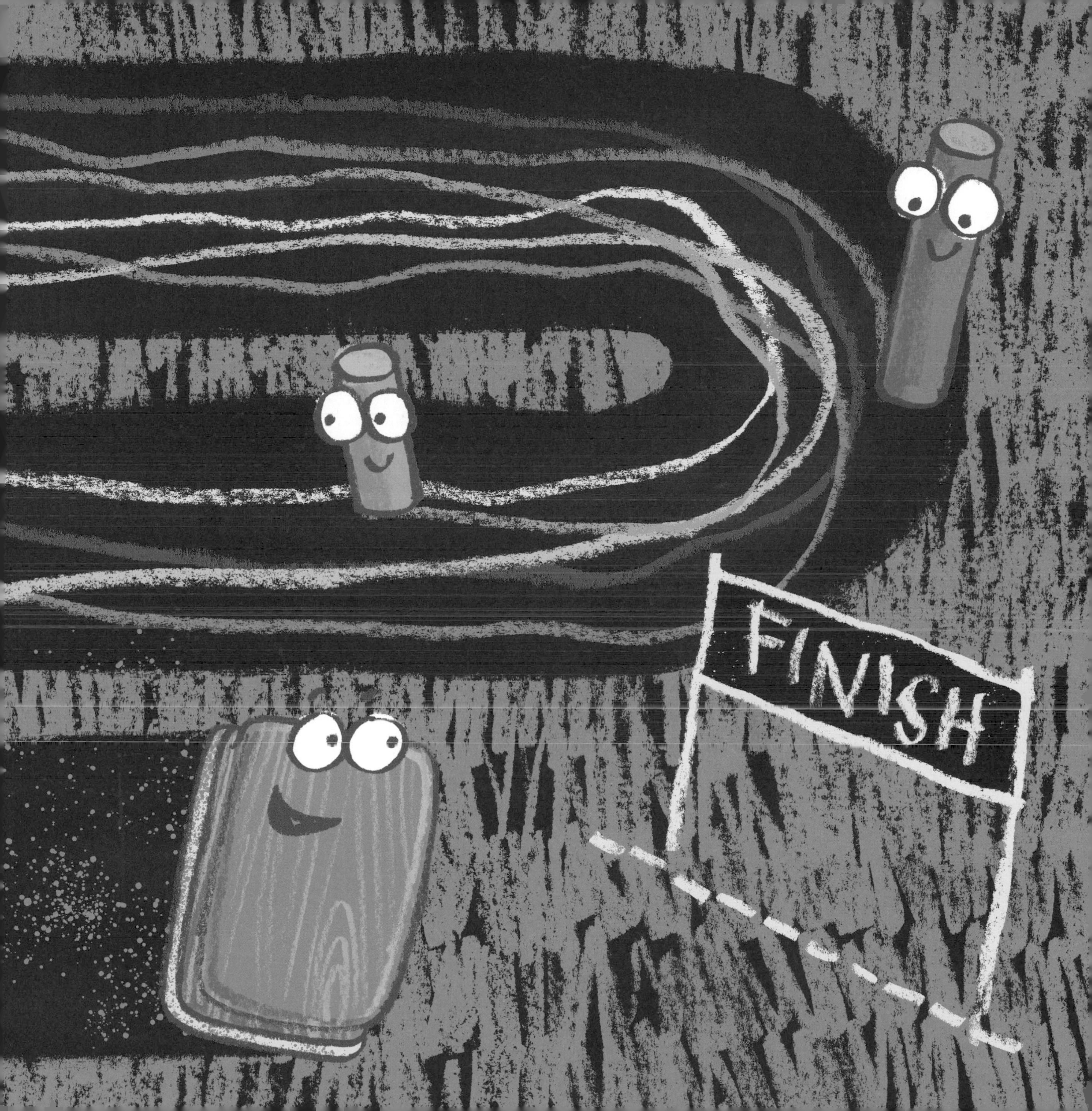
FINISH

1st